A PATCH OF SKYE

A PATCH OF SKYE

S.R. HARRIS

Illustrated by Gill Barrett

S&F

PUBLISHED BY
S&F

Uig, Isle of Skye
Landsroemlaan 24, 1083 Brussels
Tel. 00 32 2 428 62 04 Fax 00 32 2 428 05 00
E-mail: sf@scotflanders.com

First published 2006

Printed and bound in Belgium
by Atlanta, Diest.

British Library Cataloguing in Publication Data
A catalogue record for this book is
available from the British Library.

ISBN 90 76875 04 9

For Erik and the girls

IN THE GENES

Hello there, do you remember me?

I've been a Sheep On The Run these last few years but now that the Foot and Mouth virus is over we decided it would be safe to return to the Isle of Skye. And I can't tell you how glad I am to be back in my valley again, with my family. All five of us.

Five? Yes, that's right. Let me introduce you to us all again. There's me, Skye, and Jacob of course, my beloved companion. Then there's our daughter Jacuzzi with her partner Owen, who've decided to build an organic life here together. And then there is Ben, the newest of us all.

Let me tell you about Ben. Ben is not what other people expect. He wasn't what I was

Ben was almost entirely dark brown except for a few rough blotches of black splattered across his back.

expecting either. You see, I grew bigger and bigger and everyone thought I was going to have twins, or even triplets. So you can imagine mine and everyone's surprise when the time came for me to give birth and it turned out there was only ONE large brown woolly lamb inside me. Everyone kept waiting for more but that was it. That was Ben. Ben was born big.

Whereas Jacuzzi had been all dizzy little dots of brown and white, Ben was almost entirely dark brown except for a few rough blotches of black splattered across his back. He had the thickest, lumpiest wool I'd ever seen. I felt slightly alarmed when he was born. He looked so different. It was as if there was nothing in him that I could recognize.

'Who, may I ask, is that?' sneered a snooty ram with curly horns. 'A new species?'

'Doesn't look like you at all,' observed one sheep. 'Or Jacob, for that matter.'

A group of ewes sniggered quietly. 'Don't look right if you ask me,' murmured a snow white lamb, her wool brushed neatly into little curls.

I closed my eyes and imagined bits and pieces of me and Jacob floating around like lost laundry and ending up draped haphazardly over Ben in a patchwork of jackets and jeans.

'Excuse me,' said Owen solemnly. 'That is because he's made up of a different combination of genes.'

Jeans? Owen is very clever but I can't always follow him.

'Genes are what you inherit from your parents. They affect a lamb's colour, weight, the thickness of the wool. But they come in all sorts of combinations. That is why you can get a lamb that looks totally different to his parents.'

The other sheep stared at him. I was getting distinctly confused.

'What I'm trying to say,' said Owen, clearing his throat, 'is that sheep often come in various shades according to the different genes they inherit. It is quite normal.'

I closed my eyes and imagined bits and pieces of me and Jacob floating around like lost laundry and ending up draped haphazardly over Ben in a patchwork of jackets and jeans. When I opened them again I saw him quite differently. I knew just who he was. One big blob of a Ben with here and there a sprinkle of Jacob and inside him somewhere a tiny patch of Skye.

'You don't have to look like anyone but yourself,' I whispered, nuzzling him gently. 'You're unique.'

IN THE AIR

But Ben didn't only look different. He acted differently.

'Why isn't he getting up and eating like the rest?' demanded an exhausted ewe whose triplets were already driving her to distraction with their sucking.

'He's very slow,' remarked a new mother whose two lambs, barely a day old, were already frolicking skittishly behind her.

'What's the hurry?' I retorted crossly. 'He's got his whole life ahead of him.'

I didn't like anyone to criticize. But secretly I did worry. You just couldn't hurry him. Ben took his time with everything. He got up slowly, he ate slowly, he walked slowly, he bleated slowly. Sometimes he was so slow I thought one day he might come to a complete standstill.

But this time it was Jacob who helped me understand. We were lying together in the heather. 'Look.' He nodded at Ben.

He sat there very still with his ears pricked forward and his nose in the air. I saw a sheep pass, tutting to herself. I admit he did look a bit strange, as if his head wasn't screwed on properly.

'Whatever is he doing?' I sighed.

'He's listening,' whispered Jacob.

I looked at him. Ben's eyes were slightly closed. He appeared to be in a trance. I peered up at the vast expanse of sky stretching above us, like a huge beige carpet. There didn't seem to be anything in it.

'But what can he be listening to?' I asked bewildered. 'There's nothing up there.'

Jacob laughed. 'The sky is full of life,' he said. 'Clouds, insects, birds …'

I thought of the groups of tourists trekking over the hills with their cameras, getting excited about the corncrake and muddling up

Just at that moment a skylark swooped through the air and fluttered down in front of Ben's nose.

the buzzard with the golden eagle. But then people are strange like that. But us sheep, well, sheep and birds have lived together for as long as anyone can remember and we've never taken very much notice of each other at all.

'What I'm trying to say,' said Jacob, 'is that Ben is busy noticing things that the rest of us don't see.'

I looked at him. Ben had cocked his head to one side and was listening intently and suddenly I could hear it too. A warbling, a tremor of bird song carried in the wind.

And just at that moment a skylark swooped through the air and fluttered down in front of Ben's nose.

THE COMPANY OF BIRDS

Birds flocked to Ben and his thick wool provided the perfect place for them to perch. The other sheep looked on in disdain.

'If you ask me he's more bird than sheep.' A ewe sniggered from behind. 'Bird-sheep!'

'Well we didn't,' snapped Jacuzzi. She was always the first to defend her brother.

'Strange sort of ram, which prefers birds to its own kind,' the ewe continued, throwing a reproachful glance in Ben's direction. As usual Ben was lying a little way away from the others, surrounded by skylarks and starlings. She shook her head disapprovingly. 'He should stick to his own sort. It's not normal.'

But Ben wasn't normal. He liked birds and

Birds flocked to Ben and his thick wool provided the perfect place for them to perch.

the birds liked him. He listened to their songs and learned things from them that other sheep had no idea about. Things they wouldn't have been interested in anyway. They had a very low opinion of feathered creatures.

'Bird-brain,' the other sheep would hiss at him disparagingly. 'That's what comes when you mix with fowls.' They screwed up their noses as if there was a nasty smell in the air.

'It's birds that sing and sheep that bleat and never the two should mix,' said one tight-lipped ewe, shaking her head vigorously at the state the world had got itself into. 'This sort of behaviour goes right against our very nature.'

I must admit I was getting a little worried myself. I'm all for being friendly with different creatures but Ben seemed to be becoming a bird sanctuary. Various breeds had taken to resting on his back, the whinchat, the twite, the meadow pipit, all trying out their different tunes. It was very noisy and some of the older generation were complaining it was disturbing their afternoon nap. No wonder Ben was never able to hear us when we called. Sometimes I even thought I heard him bleating along with them in a strange sort of hum. I didn't know what to think.

'Calm down, Mum,' said Jacuzzi patiently. 'It's great when different creatures get together. Share their talents. Pool their resources. Produce new sounds.'

I decided to broach the subject with Jacob. But instead of taking it seriously he burst out laughing.

'Skye, have you forgotten the thoughtwaves?'

'Of course not!'

Thoughtwaves are something I discovered long ago when I went on my first journey away from the Isle of Skye. You see, we sheep don't need mobiles or computers or even the postal system. We can just think of each other and our thoughts travel directly to the one we are thinking about. It's faster than a text message and we don't even have to put a stamp on it. I must say I haven't had to use thoughtwaves for a while now but I know they are always there when needed, wrapped up safely in my wool.

'D'you remember how the other sheep reacted? They didn't like the sound of them because they were something new. They were afraid. And fear makes us do funny things. Well, now you are being just like them.'

'Am I? But this is different.'

'No it's not. It's just another form of thoughtwaves. But this time it's between birds and sheep.'

I hadn't looked at it like that. I glanced across at Ben and saw him surrounded by skylarks and dunlins and greenshanks pecking at his ears, nestling into his wool, all chirruping their different melodies. And somewhere above them I could just make out the plaintive whistle of the Golden Plover tumbling through the air. Never mind what all the other sheep were saying. They were frightened because it was different. Now Jacob had taken the fear out of my eyes I was able to see how happy they looked and how beautiful it was.

I'd caught the other sheep peering at me during the mother and baby's wool-combing sessions ...

HIDE AND SEEK

But it wasn't easy for Ben. Some of the other lambs had been told by their mothers to avoid going too near him.

'We never know what he might have picked up,' hissed a fussy little ewe, dusting down her daughter's back. 'There's bird flu all over the place these days. And have you seen the state of his wool?'

I had tried but it was almost impossible to brush Ben's coat. It was so thick and tangly, and everywhere he went pieces of bracken and goodness knows what got stuck in it. I'd caught the other sheep peering at me during the mother and baby's wool-combing sessions when I was trying to untangle a particularly sticky knot and tut-tutting over their shoulders.

'How difficult it must be to keep him clean,' a Cheviot had smirked.

'So unfortunate he's such a naturally dirty colour,' a Whiteface with spotless twins remarked. 'I believe it's possible these days to do something about it. There's a wonderful range of dyes on the market now.'

'He's a lovely colour and I wouldn't change it for anything,' I retorted. 'Besides, it suits the landscape.'

'It certainly does,' laughed another. 'It's the colour of mud.'

There was a lot of speculation among the sheep community as to the exact nature of Ben's ailments. Many were convinced it ran in the family.

'Like mother, like son,' I heard a ewe whispering behind my wool. 'Take that Skye for example. She's a bed and breakfast case. Never even knew her own mother. And think what happened to Jacuzzi! Wandering off to the other ends of the earth. It's in the blood.' Her eyes narrowed and she leant forward, mouthing dramatically, spit positively frothing at her mouth. 'Bad Blood Will Out.'

'Whatever it is, one can never be too careful,' said another mum emphatically, busy twisting her lamb's wool into tight little curls. 'These things can be catching. Stand still, dear, for goodness sake, I've half your back to do yet. I'm certainly not letting my Bonnie play with him.' The others bleated in agreement.

Ben pretended that he didn't mind. He had the company of birds and he could do without the silliness of sheep. But it made him feel sad. He would have liked to play with the other lambs. Ben loved games. His favourite was hide and seek. The only sheep who played with him were Jacuzzi and Owen and they were often too busy discussing the future of the planet and drawing up plans for their organic garden. Owen wasn't very good at games anyway. He liked things to have a point to them so he preferred drawing up lists of plants and complicated attributes like perfectly rounded stones and seagull feathers that they needed for their gardening project

One even sneaked up behind him and tweaked a piece of his wool until he yelped with pain.

and giving them to Ben to find.

He liked that. He was good at finding things. He always managed to collect everything that was on Owen's list, and a lot of items that weren't. Wherever he went all sorts of things would cling to his wool. Sticks, flowers, strips of plastic, pieces of wire. The other lambs skipped about together a little distance away, giggling at Ben's matted coat full of strange objects. One even sneaked up behind him and tweaked a piece of his wool until he yelped with pain.

'What d'you do that for?' Ben turned round sharply.

'I just wanted to see if it was real,' he said.

'Of course it's real. Why wouldn't it be?'

'Because you're not like us. My Dad says you've got a screw loose ...' said the bold little lamb importantly. 'That's why you talk to the birds.'

Ben shrugged. 'Why won't you play with me?' he asked.

'My Mum won't let me.'

'Why not?'

'You're not all there.' He shook his head disparagingly. 'You're missing a gene.'

LOST PROPERTY

That's when Ben started wandering off on his own. As you know I'm pretty used to that. But whereas Jacuzzi used to go to the other side of the valley, Ben was drawn to the mountains, just like his name. Ben comes from the Gaelic *Beann*, meaning mountain peak. It used to worry me at first but Owen assured me that Ben had got a very good sense of direction. I nodded wisely. Probably something to do with a compass in his jeans. But I understood Jacuzzi better.

'Don't worry, Mum. If I was lost up there, I'd rather be with Ben than anyone else,' she said, giving me a reassuring nuzzle.

And she was right. He came to know the mountains better than any of us. Ben Edra was his favourite. From here it looks like a huge slab of barren moorland but to Ben it became a place of infinite variety and endless surprises. He discovered trees that grew from rocks, water that murmured under the earth, insects that buzzed in the bracken. In the most desolate of places he came across tiny signs of life: carpets of golden saxifrage, sprigs of juniper berries, clumps of bog cotton, primroses peeping through stones. He stumbled on to ledges where the fulmars made their nest, the crags where the buzzard perched, the cliff where the osprey sheltered. He reached waterfalls that thundered down slopes as sheer as glass and drank from pools as clear as tear drops. He shared his secrets with the mountain and the mountain shared its secrets with him.

And there was always so much to find even if it wasn't what he was looking for. He would appear on the horizon, slowly descending the slope, with all kinds of treasures hidden in his wool. He found wild thyme for Owen's herb garden and brought me a four-leaf clover

Not to mention all the left-hand gloves and woolly hats and single socks that he's picked up.

wrapped inside a sprig of white heather. Once he picked up an intriguing bottle called 'midge milk' which still had something in it but which left a strange scented taste in one's mouth. Another time he returned with two tiny gold earrings which he gave to Jacuzzi, but they were so small that one of them got lost inside her ear.

It's amazing what gets left behind in the mountains. Bits of string, matchboxes, sweet papers, tins, hairbands, even jewellery. Not to mention all the left-hand gloves and woolly hats and single socks that he's picked up. I always hang them on the fence in case their owner comes along but so far nobody has collected them. They just end up staying there, waving to us in the wind. Once Ben found a clock which he gave to Jacob, but the ticking made us nervous so we hid it in a rabbit hole. We didn't tell him in case he found it for us again. Another time he returned with a torch. We all rallied round excitedly but unfortunately we couldn't make it work.

'Flat batteries,' explained Owen. 'They're not rechargeable.' He shook his head disapprovingly.

And then, one day, he brought back a bird with a broken wing.

'She was lying in the heather, beside the waterfall,' he explained.

We stared at the skylark who was starting to chirrup plaintively. She didn't look very happy.

'What will you do with her?' I asked.

'She can live with me,' said Ben. 'Till she gets better. There's plenty of room on my back.'

'But a bird is used to being up in the sky. It likes air, not wool.' I peered down dubiously at the little creature nestling in Ben's coat. It could be in danger of suffocating.

'I'll take her with me when I go up to the mountains,' said Ben doggedly. 'She'll like it up there. It's the closest I can get to the sky.'

So Ben continued his treks. If you looked up into the hills you could often make out the familiar outline of the sheep with the skylark

If you looked up into the hills you could often make out the familiar outline of the sheep with the skylark on his back.

on his back, trawling the landscape, like a solitary beacon on the horizon. Gradually he built up a reputation as a mobile lost-property office. If any of us was looking for anything we would always say 'Where's Ben? He'll find it for you.' Because Jacob was right. Ben saw the things that we didn't see.

TIPSY'S TALE

The days were lengthening and summer was in sight. Our valley, which is so deserted for most of the year, was now visited by people in large walking boots carrying an enormous amount of luggage. You would be amazed how much human beings take with them when they go walking. It makes me glad I'm a sheep with just my own wool on my back. Anyway, summer is the time of the backpackers and that meant a lot of work for Ben. He always kept track of who was up on the mountain and which path they had taken. And of course, there were a lot more things to find. If you take so much with you there's always so much to lose. And lose things they did.

The skylark always went with him because she still wasn't able to fly. Privately we were wondering if she would ever fly again. Perhaps she preferred to be carried forever, wrapped up in Ben's blanket of thick, warm wool.

But Ben knew it wasn't like that. The skylark had told him her story and he carried her secret around with him. Before her accident she had been known as Tiptoe the tightrope walker because she was always hopping along telegraph wires and balancing on the top of cliffs. Apparently she had once been able to hang upside down from electricity cables and do somersaults in the air. She could even juggle with feathers at the same time. Ever since she was a chick she had loved gymnastics, exercising every day. Over time she had become fearless. She would practise her performances until she had split-second timing, perfect balance. In the bird world she built up quite a name for herself. She became a high flyer spiralling up into the clouds, performing tricks in the air. The sky

She could even juggle with feathers at the same time.

was her stage. Birds used to come from all over to see her. Even a flock of geese on their way south would stop off to watch the show.

But then one day something happened. She was performing her most difficult trick on the highest waterfall below Ben Edra and there was a row of birds watching her from the bottom of the cliff. Even a few puffins had turned up this time. She looked down and saw the rocks and the water thundering below her and she felt something she had never felt before. A cold feeling that froze her feathers. And suddenly she lost her balance. Instead of soaring gracefully into the air she hurtled flat against the rock in front of her and the next thing she knew she was lying in the middle of a bog with a damaged wing. She was so ashamed she hid herself in the heather until all the birds had disappeared. It was easy to hide because her plumage blended into the landscape. They must have presumed she was dead. She only survived because she was spotted by a flock of seagulls who took pity on her for a while and brought her pieces of

She was performing her most difficult trick on the highest waterfall below Ben Edra and there was a row of birds watching her from the bottom of the cliff.

fish. But every time she tried to get up she kept falling over so they laughed at her and called her Tipsy. 'So that's who I became,' she said, shaking her feathers sadly.

Although her wing was almost healed, every time she tried to take off into the air, that same rock came hurtling into view, knocking her off course and all she could hear was the roar of the water crashing beneath her and a loud buzzing sound filled her ears. Something cold would grip her wings and her feathers would begin to shake and she would turn dizzy and start to fall.

'I've lost my balance,' she confided sadly. 'I'll never be Tiptoe again. A bird that can't fly isn't a proper bird. I don't belong in the air any more.' She looked up wistfully.

'We'll keep on looking for it,' said Ben reassuringly, thinking of the missing gene that still eluded him. 'And one day we'll find it. In the meantime you can belong in the hills with me. We've both lost bits of ourselves.' He shrugged. 'We suit each other.'

SAVING THE PLANET

There were things Ben and Tipsy were looking for that they couldn't find, but there were plenty of things that they found that they weren't looking for. And which nobody else was looking for either. When Ben got back he would slowly unload the objects off his back and put them in a pile on the ground. One glove, half a biscuit, a piece of sticking plaster, an empty milk bottle. We would all stare at them and every day a little group of sheep would come nosing around to see if anything Ben had found was of any use to them. It never was. Privately I thought this quaint collection of objects looked rather sad. Everything was either lost or incomplete or empty. And each day the pile grew bigger.

'It's as if all these things have got nothing to do with each other,' I said to Owen dejectedly, as I tried to pair up two totally different gloves. 'Except that Ben found them.'

Owen stared at me thoughtfully. 'There's no system, that's why.' His face lit up. 'We need to create one. We need to start sorting.' He began rummaging around, putting all the cartons to one side. 'It's called recycling,' he said excitedly. Not many sheep, except for Owen, could have got excited about something like this. 'This is the future. The resources of the world are not inexhaustible.'

It took us a while to get our system right. I would have preferred to sort according to colours but Owen didn't think that a very scientific approach. So biscuit wrappers went together with newspapers, snippets of wire with iron pegs, gloves and socks with scraps of tent, pieces of glass with wine bottles and plastic bags together with library cards. 'It depends on what material they are made of,' explained Owen patiently.

'And what now?' I enquired gloomily, surveying the row of piles. They still looked sad, even if they were now with their own kind.

'We must either make something else out of them or carry them to containers at the pier.'

'Won't that take rather a long time?' I asked glumly, imagining countless treks down the hill with one or two useless plastic objects buried in our wool.

'We have time,' said Owen philosophically. 'But the planet doesn't. Anyway we could form a chain ...' His eyes brightened. I could see he was imagining a production line of sheep passing bottles to each other all the way down to Uig Pier.

'Anyway that is only for the things we can't recycle ourselves. Our first priority is to give these objects a new life.'

I peered down at the empty bottles, wondering whatever we could make out of them.

'For example you could unravel the

woollen articles and knit us all slippers for the winter. You know how cold our feet get in the snow.'

'Oh, so I could,' I said without much enthusiasm. I wondered how many slippers I could make out of five gloves and seven socks and whether I would manage to finish even one pair before the winter set in.

'It might take years,' I ventured wearily.

'No problem,' said Owen encouragingly. He could be maddeningly cheerful at times. 'We have to look at things in the long term. We may not see the fruit of our labour but our children will, or our children's children.'

Oh dear. I could imagine myself knitting for ever.

PART OF A PLAN

The other sheep sniggered at our efforts.

'Not a very useful occupation, is it?' sneered one of the rams as he watched Jacuzzi unravelling wool from a piece of barbed wire.

'More useful than eating grass,' she retorted.

'Never,' said the ram, pulling himself up to his full height, 'denigrate the calling of a sheep. The purpose of a sheep is to graze. Grazing is a very respectable activity.' He raised his horns dramatically. 'I'll have you know that people even pay good money for machines that graze. They are called lawn-mowers. You can find them in every reputable do-it-yourself shop.' He sniffed.

'Yes, but there are hundreds of lawn-mowers and very few recycling businesses like ours,' said Jacuzzi. I shot her a grateful look. Jacuzzi was a fighter and, unlike me, she always knew what to say next.

'What a terrible mess! What IS the point of all this?' exclaimed a nervous little sheep, standing a little way away, who was obviously afraid of getting her wool dirty. I'd secretly wanted to ask that myself but hadn't liked to. Owen seemed so purposeful I was sure it must be just me who was missing the point. I stared down at the haphazard array of broken objects lying around us. I rather wished Ben had left them all where he'd found them. I'm sure they would rot away in the end. It seemed all this recycling was making the earth messier, not the other way round.

'I don't know why you bother.' A large ram gulped down the last of his grass sandwich and belched contentedly. 'This is work for humans, not sheep. If I were you I'd leave this to them. They are the ones who created the problem in the first place.'

'We can all play our part,' said Owen stoically.

'We do, just by being who we are. We sheep are an ecological example to the human race.'

'Yes, well, some of us like to do more than just BE,' said Jacuzzi impatiently. 'And if you don't mind could you help me by holding this wire for a moment?'

'I'm afraid I am otherwise engaged. I rather fancy another green salad.'

'That's not very helpful,' grumbled Jacuzzi.

'My dear, that's where you are wrong,' said the ram importantly. 'Eating is very productive. We sheep are recyclable. We re-enter the food chain. Grass to grass, earth to earth. Be a sheep and save the world.' He waddled off, chuckling to himself.

I was half inclined to agree. Perhaps we should just concentrate on being sheep. It would be a lot less tiring. But Owen's eyes were gleaming. My heart sank. They looked like eyes with a plan. I hoped he wasn't planning too much. I wasn't sure if Owen had the hang of a sheep's life. In a sheep's life there is not a lot of space for a plan.

'We are involved here in an experiment,' explained Owen. 'An ecological experiment. Its purpose may not be completely clear to us at the moment because it is ahead of its time. But you can be sure it is of great symbolic significance. Think of it as a candle in the dark.'

I looked down at the motley selection of objects lying dejectedly in small piles. Perhaps they weren't so useless after all. They were part of a plan. I picked up a left glove and rubbed it gently against my cheek. 'You've got a whole new life ahead of you,' I whispered, trying not to think of all the knitting it would take. A candle in the dark. I closed my eyes. It sounded lovely.

I was busy with the unravelling of knitted garments and Jacuzzi's job was washing out the bottles.

THE MOBILE

And so our little business flourished insomuch as there was always something that Ben brought back and therefore always something for us to sort. Owen did the initial sorting as he was the one who could identify the materials best. He seemed to have shelved his organic gardening project for the moment so he could concentrate completely on recycling the planet. I was busy with the unravelling of knitted garments and Jacuzzi's job was washing out the bottles. We also had an impressive collection of bones and skeletons that Jacob was collecting and sorting. He had decided to break up the smoothest ones so they could be used for the game of jacks. Owen suggested the others could be displayed like a small museum so that we could all see what we were going to turn into in the end but I wasn't sure how many of us really wanted to know. Ben, of course, was the finder and gatherer, trawling the mountains with the skylark chirupping in his ear.

'D'you think it's all worth it?' Jacob asked me one evening. I was busy tying myself up in knots trying to undo all this wool and it was making me decidedly dizzy. I closed my eyes for a moment and tried to get my bearings. When I opened them again I noticed how tired Jacob looked. It wasn't like him to get disheartened. Being with bones all day was obviously taking its toll. I stroked his cheek.

'We're all working together now. We've got a common goal and each has their part to play. And look at Ben! He's always on the outside and nobody wants him to join in. But here he's at the heart of it all.' I squeezed Jacob's hoof and nuzzled myself against him. 'You always make a difference to me,' I said. 'But now you're making a difference to the planet too.'

One evening Ben returned with something small and black wrapped up in his wool. 'Look what I've found!' he said, shaking it free.

It was a tiny bleeping machine with a screen the shape of an ear tag.

'I heard it singing in the heather,' said Ben. 'We thought it must be a new species of bird but then it stopped and started bleeping instead.'

'That's a mobile,' said Jacob.

'Which pile?' I asked dubiously.

'Technology,' said Owen excitedly. 'This belongs to a new category.'

'Couldn't we put it with bottles for the moment?' The piles were confusing enough as it was and starting a new one only added to the chaos.

'Soon there will be more,' he said. 'This is the pile of the future.'

He was examining it closely when the tune 'Scotland the Brave' suddenly burst out of it. Jacuzzi grabbed hold of Ben's wool and they

'Technology,' said Owen excitedly. 'This belongs to a new category.'

started dancing. Owen frowned.

'Shouldn't we answer it?' I asked anxiously.

'We're sheep,' Jacob said. 'Sheep don't answer mobile phones.'

'But what if it's an emergency?'

We stared at it uncertainly until the ringing stopped and we couldn't answer it anyway. A few moments later it started to bleep.

'That's a message coming in,' said Jacob. I gazed at him in admiration. How clever he was to know all that.

'What does it say?' We all crowded round excitedly.

'It says ... ' Jacob squinted down at the text. 'Jack, where are you? Please phone me. Julie.'

'We ought to do something,' said Jacuzzi. 'She sounds worried.'

'She'd be much more worried if she got a phone call from a sheep,' answered Jacob.

Ben was staring up at the mountains. 'There were five who went out this morning. And only four came back,' he murmured.

Ben always noticed the number of backpackers he came across on the mountains. He always knew how many of them were out each day and which path they had taken and where they were heading for.

'The last one was alone.' Ben frowned. 'He wasn't like the others. He didn't take much with him.'

'He probably returned by a different route,' said Jacuzzi hopefully.

A moment later the phone beeped again.

'I'm worried. Please text me. Ju xxxx'

I liked the kisses at the end. I sniffed the screen and my nose tickled.

'I'm going to look for him,' said Ben.

THE RIDGE

We knew better than to dissuade him. If anyone could find a lost person it would be Ben. And the mobile was getting frantic. It kept on bleeping more and more messages. We wished we could send one back saying Ben was going to find him but our hooves were too big to press the right letters.

'We'll look after the mobile,' I said, gazing at it reverently.

Jacob shook his head. 'Ben must take it with him so he can give it to Jack. Then he can send a reply.'

Of course! I felt suitably chastened. I wished I'd thought of that.

We wrapped the little black machine carefully in Ben's wool and said goodbye. We

And when he turned we all nodded and a tear trickled down my nose and landed in my wool.

all stood in a line watching him and the mobile and the skylark make their ascent up the mountain. And when he turned we all nodded and a tear trickled down my nose and landed in my wool. I felt so proud of him. My beautiful Ben, the odd-bod, the bird-sheep, was setting off into the darkness to look for more lost property.

Ben trudged up the track towards the ridge. Soon it would disappear completely and there would be just bog and moorland. That's what he liked best of all. The wilderness. Clump after clump of purple heather, their dark roots matted like tangled hair. Ahead of him a river twisted snake-like through the glen and he caught a glimpse of its silver tail. A person should be easy to find because he left tracks. Footprints squelching through mud, lumps of heather flattened by heavy boots, the odd piece of litter. But it was getting dark and the tracks were harder to make out. He had a feeling that the man had probably made for the ridge, the point where the sea came into view. Humans are always hoping for something beyond the next horizon.

In his wool the phone kept bleeping away. 'More messages,' Tipsy chirped. She cradled the phone in her feathers to keep it warm and stop it from worrying. Sometimes it sang, sometimes it hummed. In the end it went quiet as if it had given up the struggle completely.

Ben sniffed the air. It was becoming colder, there could even be a frost tonight. He sensed a change in the atmosphere. Dusk was fading into darkness. Soon the night would fall like a blanket wiping out the distractions of the day. Even the sheep would stop munching and everything would withdraw into darkness and close its eyes. Each part of the day had a different colour. The night was purple and black like a bruise that needed time to heal. Dawn was a silver gift, another chance, the world was new, pearls of dew glittering on blades of grass. Midday was the brightest when the grass was at its greenest and a sheep was simply a sheep. The middle of the day was green. Dusk was grey and pink, the twilight zone, full of shadows, the blurring of the lines between past and present, the merging of time. Occasionally when the sun was low, a golden light would suffuse the landscape and the hills would glow. Ben knew that everything had its moment. Even the darkest depths of the night would give way to a time when the sky would lighten and the earth would sing again.

They had gone a long way up now and were getting tired. Ben stopped to rest by a burn and took a cold drink of peaty water. He had seen people putting up little houses on the ridge, unpacking huge parcels, rolling out bedding, settling down for the night. Humans weren't used to being out in the cold and the rain, like sheep. But if Jack had been planning on camping out here, then why was he being sent so many messages?

The ridge was always further than one thought. There was always another slope to ascend, rising unexpectedly out of the heather. Sometimes the earth crumbled away beneath his hooves, revealing a hidden cliff. Even a sheep had to be careful here. But soon they would get there. And when they did the land seemed to break away, falling down in front of them in folds. It was as if they were on top of the world. The sky was heavy with clouds but he knew that the village of Staffin lay nestled somewhere down there in the valley beneath the rocks of the Quiraing, and beyond that stretched the endless expanse of the sea.

The ridge was completely deserted. Or so it seemed. Ben trudged on up towards the summit. There had been so much rain these last days that the earth squelched beneath his hooves, making each step heavier than usual. He looked around at the desolate moorland unfolding in front of him. There were no signs of life. He began to wonder if he was ever going to find Jack. It was getting darker by the minute and the temperature was falling rapidly. These were not good conditions to be lost in.

Tipsy seemed to sense his mood.

'Don't you think we'll find him?' she whispered.

'I don't know,' he replied wearily.

'D'you think you'll ever find the thing you've lost?' She knew it was something like a jean or a joan. Or was it a john?

Ben shrugged. He had come across so many other things that he sometimes forgot what it was he had originally set out to find.

'What does it look like?' ventured Tipsy.

Ben wasn't sure. He imagined it as a kind of lozenge, the shape of a boiled sweet. That's why he had been so excited when he had once found a small sheet of pills set out in a row, each one wrapped up separately in silver foil.

He had tried one eagerly but it had made him choke and he had only just managed to swallow it. It hadn't changed him at all so it can't have been his missing gene. Jacuzzi had told him afterwards that they were cough tablets. Strange how they ended up giving you a cough instead of taking it away.

'Why d'you want to find it anyway?' asked Tipsy.

'So I'll become like the others and they'll let me play with them.' Ben sighed. It sounded impossible even to his own ears.

'Don't despair, Benny. There are places where everything is found,' whispered Tipsy, tickling his nose with her feathers.

Ben had heard of such places. He had learned from the birds that there are lines in the landscape, places where the worlds merge and the air becomes thin. These are not places that earthbound creatures like people and sheep ever get to. But birds dip in and out of these different zones and bring back the evidence: feathers, stories, songs that they've heard there. There are places which, when you leave, you can't explain where you've been, a swallow had once told him. Places of silver. Mist. Light. Where you are lifted up. Carried. Where you can touch the earth's face.

Ben had never been to such a place but if he stayed very still and listened very carefully he sometimes caught wind of something in the air. An echo. The notes of a song so beautiful it made him cry. And once, when he had been up in the mountains and night was falling and he had felt as if he was the only living creature left in the world, he had heard someone calling his name, very softly, like a whisper in the wind. He had lain down in the cold heather and closed his eyes. It was as if the earth was breathing beside him and he was no longer alone. It had made him feel safe.

He didn't like to talk to the other sheep about these things. He knew from experience that sheep could be very short-sighted. They look around them and all they see is grass. They would either laugh and think he was

'So he went this way,' I heard one of them say. He was frowning at a map.

imagining things or taunt him for trying to be too clever for his own good. Stick with your own kind and keep your head down is their motto. They are wary of crossing boundaries into other creatures' worlds. It was better to keep secrets like this wrapped up safely in his own wool.

They were reaching the summit now. At the top was a lump of stones. Was one of these placed by Jack? There was no indication that he had passed this way but then signs were easily eradicated. Footprints disappeared. Stones moved all the time. The landscape was changing by the minute but it happened so slowly you only noticed it after thousands of years.

Down in the valley a jeep had arrived, bumping along the track with its headlights blazing. When it couldn't get any further it stopped and two large men with torches got out. A girl scrambled after them. 'So he went this way,' I heard one of them say. He was frowning at a map. I noticed that he had a little mobile with him with a bleeping screen just like the one Ben had found. But this time it sang a different song, 'The Bluebells of Scotland'.

'Did he have a compass?' The man turned to the girl who was trying to stop herself shivering. She shook her head.

'He wasn't well equipped at all. He left just like that.'

'You mustn't worry too much, lass. He'll be all right. He's a young man.'

The girl shook her head. 'You don't understand. He wasn't in a good state of mind when he set off this morning. He'd sort of … lost hope.'

'Try his number again,' one of them said. I thought of the phone ringing away in Ben's wool.

'No coverage,' he muttered, shaking his head. 'I'm afraid there's no reaching him tonight. We'll have to wait till tomorrow. We'll set out on a search party at first light and request the mountain rescue to send out a helicopter.' They got back into the warmth of their jeep, the girl following reluctantly, and roared off leaving a chilly silence behind them.

I looked up at the mountains disappearing into the darkness. There was so much you could lose. Jeans, socks, hope. Could all those things be found up there? I shivered. I just hoped Ben would be all right.

'You could always send him a thoughtwave,' Jacob said. 'You don't need coverage for that.'

Ben could feel Tipsy tightening her grip.

THE WATERFALL

Ben was resting on a ledge just below the summit when the thoughtwave arrived. It took the weariness out of his wool and the heaviness from his hooves and he suddenly remembered the way I had looked at him when he had set out. I had been proud of him. I had believed in him. He wrapped the phone up in his wool to keep it warm and stop the battery from buzzing and it now gave a contented little sigh as if it had decided to sleep. A little way away Tipsy was perched on a rock practising her balance.

'Let's move on,' said Ben, perking up suddenly. 'I have an idea.'

In the distance Ben could hear the rush of water against rock. Far above him a buzzard swooped and circled. So far he had kept away from the waterfall for Tipsy's sake because he didn't want to upset her. He was afraid it would bring back bad memories. But the idea was leading him towards it now. He had a feeling this would be the place. A place you are drawn to. A place of awe and beauty. A place on the edge where you can lose your balance, put your life at risk.

Ben had learned a lot from the mountains. Mountains had a history. They had been there long before sheep came along and they would be there long after sheep had gone. He had learned from the mountains that you sometimes had to sit things out. He used to be scared out in the wilderness alone when night fell. There were all these shapes. But he had learned not to run away. If you turn away from the shadow it becomes bigger but if you walk into it you can't tell any more where it begins and where it ends. You become a part of that shape. It loses its strangeness. It becomes closer to you than your own wool.

The roar got louder, like thunder, and he

knew they were nearly there. Ben could feel Tipsy tightening her grip. A light mist had fallen and through the gloaming Ben could just make out the spray of the water as it crashed against the rock. He stopped and stared. Something bright and red lay almost buried under a clump of heather. When he got closer it turned into a woolly hat. It looked as if it had been abandoned. Could it have belonged to Jack? And, if so, maybe he was somewhere near by.

Ben started to bleat. Maybe if Jack heard some living creature he would respond. But maybe he couldn't. Maybe something terrible had happened to him.

The phone had stopped bleeping and Tipsy had stopped singing. There was an ominous silence in the air. He looked round at her. The colour had drained from her feathers and she was trembling. 'It was here,' she whispered.

Ben nodded. But he couldn't turn back now. They would have to sit it out. Together. Jack couldn't be far from here.

Tipsy had curled herself up into a ball in his wool.

'You have to help me,' said Ben. 'You have to sing.'

She was silent.

'Please. He needs to hear you sing.'

'I can't, Ben.'

'You can. It will help us find him.'

'I've lost my voice,' she croaked.

'Try, Tipsy. Please try. Do it for me.'

So Tipsy began to sing, slowly and shakily at first and then stronger and clearer until it filled the air with song and the silence melted away.

TIPTOE

They headed to the base of the waterfall. The drop was too sheer to negotiate directly so Ben had to make a detour along the hill. The waterfalls here made deep gashes in the landscape. He picked his way down carefully, resting in ledges on the way. Luckily he was used to heights but his hooves still slithered on the slippery turf and he had to keep his gaze fixed on the route ahead. If he lost his foothold he wouldn't find another.

Rocks have a face and this one was grim and forbidding. Water roared and gulped down its cheeks. Lumps of stone protruded like warts from its forehead. When the wind caught the spray it created an eddy of tiny waterfalls trickling down its dark neck. It was dangerous to fall into its clutches. There was nothing to break his fall. No trees sticking their limbs out to wave at him, only a few tufts of grass as tough as an old man's beard.

The roar was deafening now and not even Tipsy could make her voice heard. Every cry for help would be drowned in its torrent. Every so often they were drenched in a sheet of spray. Ben knew you had to be careful with water. When it's angry it can whip your face, sting your wool, swallow you whole. Here it was frothing at the mouth, transformed into a seething mass of brown, boiling liquid. But further afield it would turn into a meandering river, trickling and murmuring through the landscape, soft and sustaining. In the flat basin of the valley cattle grazed peacefully among the ruins of the old village, the waterfall reduced to a faint humming like the hiss of cars on a distant motorway.

They were reaching the bottom now. Ben tripped over a pile of scattered bones. He shivered and looked around him hesitantly. He noticed a bunch of thistles, their flowers bobbing in the wind like purple berets, pushing their way up through a motley assortment of jagged stones. And what was that over there? Through the darkness Ben could make out something lying on the ground near the waterfall. A dark shape.

Ben hurried towards it, his heart sinking. As he got closer the shape turned itself into a man. He was lying with his head half hidden in a clump of bracken. He didn't look hurt but there was something about the way he was positioned that made it seem as if he had simply collapsed on the ground and gone to sleep. His arms hung dejectedly by his side. His scarf trailed limply round his neck. His jacket wasn't even zipped up. Ben moved closer towards him. His face was pale and there were dark grooves on his cheek where he had been lying against the bracken. He was breathing slowly as if each breath was an effort. He opened his eyes and Ben and Jack came face to face with each other.

For a moment Jack's eyes were startled and then they cleared with relief. Ben bleated

Ben knew the important thing now was to keep the man warm. He would be his blanket.

softly and moved forward. He nuzzled the man's cheek. It was cold as ice. Then Ben gently let the mobile fall into the man's hand. Tiptoe sang gently into his ear. The man shook his head. Ben noticed his fingers were a bluish colour and he was shaking so much he could hardly grasp the phone. With a great effort he tried to draw himself up and press one of the numbers. But nothing happened. Something was wrong. There were no tunes any more. The phone had gone dead.

Jack lay back, the effort too much for him. Ben nestled down beside him. It was very damp down here. Just above them water dripped over a small ledge, creating dozens of tiny waterfalls splashing over their heads. He knew that people mustn't get too cold. It was different for sheep. They are always well wrapped up. They can even survive in snow for weeks on end by making an igloo and licking the ice. Ben knew the important thing now was to keep the man warm. He would be his blanket. Tipsy carried on singing very gently. The notes soared and fell, tripping sweetly through the air in contrast to the roar of the thundering water. From here Ben could see how the cliff was made up of different layers of rock with a dark red seam at the bottom. Above his head the stone was glistening with green lichen. Jack closed his eyes, clutched the phone to his chest, leant his head against Ben's back.

They must have both fallen asleep because when Ben woke Tipsy's singing sounded far away and there was a faint light emerging over the hills. Ben had wrapped himself round Jack's body as best he could in order to keep him warm and listen to his breathing. Jack had been leaning against him for hours now and Ben had become so stiff he wasn't sure if he was able to move. But he could hear Jack's heart, like a clock, ticking through his clothes. It was extremely uncomfortable being a duvet. Perhaps if he stayed here in this position long enough he would be so flat he would actually turn into one. He tried to turn his head. Tipsy didn't seem to be there any more. Wherever had she got to?

Suddenly a song burst out just above Ben's ears. He looked up and there she was fluttering above him. He couldn't believe his eyes.

'I've found it, Ben,' she said excitedly. 'My balance. Look!' She dipped down on to Ben's back and then took off again, soaring into the air, swooping up over the waterfall. Ben watched in amazement. Her movements were as graceful as a ballet dancer. She was like a tiny strip of silver streaking against the darkness of the rock face. Suddenly she was back beside Ben's nose.

'What happened?' he asked.

'I was just practising and for the first time since the accident I didn't see the rocks and the waterfall crashing all around me. D'you know what I saw instead?'

Ben shook his head.

'I saw you.'

Ben felt his wool turn warm. He didn't know where to look.

'And that's when it came back. My balance. I was able to take off. Before I knew it I was actually flying! I've found it again in the very place I lost it.' She gave two little swoops in the air. Her eyes were shining. 'Thank you, Ben,' she whispered. 'It was you who found it for me.' She hopped along his neck, making his wool tickle.

'You're Tiptoe again now,' Ben replied.

MOVING ON

They both looked at Jack. He had sat up and was staring at them strangely. Although his face was very pale and there were dark smudges under his eyes, something like a smile was forming at the corner of his lips. Surely he couldn't understand what they were saying? Perhaps he was laughing at Ben's wool, of which wisps were still clinging to his jacket. Or perhaps it was Tiptoe's gymnastics and the way she somersaulted in the air. Whatever it was the smile spread slowly over his tired face and something seemed to light up inside his eyes.

He seemed to want to make a move. He shook his head and staggered slowly to his feet. At first he appeared in a daze, as if he

He had sat up and was staring at them strangely.

was about to topple over, but then he steadied himself and set off unsteadily towards the river.

'I think we should keep an eye on him,' murmured Ben.

He hurried to overtake Jack but it was difficult to walk. Ben felt flat, as if all the life had been crushed out of his wool. Jack's body had been slumped against him for so long and it felt strange not to have Tipsy on his back. Tiptoe, he corrected himself. He felt a little sad. They had suited each other so well. Ben and Tipsy. Both odd. Both missing a vital part of themselves. Now Tipsy had found her balance again she might not want to have anything to do with a sheep like him. She surely wouldn't want to live on his back any more.

He looked around. Jack was stumbling along behind him, humming quietly. He seemed to be following. But where was Tiptoe? Wherever had she got to? Of course she could fly off now any time, he thought. A large salty tear trickled down his cheek.

'Hi!' Tiptoe had landed on top of his head and was licking his ear. 'What's the matter?'

'I'll miss you,' said Ben. 'I'll miss you on my back.'

'But I'm not going anywhere,' said Tiptoe.

'You can fly now. You've found your balance. You don't need me any more.' Ben sighed. 'You must go back to your own kind.'

'You are my own kind. My only kind.'

'But you don't want to stay with me. You're a high flyer, a wire walker, and I'm just a silly old sheep with a missing gene.'

'You're not a silly old sheep to me, Ben. Anyway, how d'you know you're missing a gene?'

'The others told me. There's something wrong with me.'

'What is wrong with you?'

'My wool's all lumpy.'

'Your wool kept Jack warm.'

'And I talk to the birds.'

'So when you find your gene your wool will go flat and you won't talk to me any more?'

'I'll always talk to you.'

'But I'm a bird.'

'Yes, well, you're different.'

Tiptoe sighed. 'And so are you. I like you that way. I don't want you to change. Your wool kept Jack alive. And if you hadn't talked to me I wouldn't have got my balance back. There's nothing missing in you. You're perfect as you are. You're complete.'

Ben's heart gave a little leap and his wool seemed to breathe again. He felt much less flat all of a sudden.

'Take no notice of what the others say,' Tiptoe whispered in his ear. 'They don't understand. They haven't done what you've done. They haven't saved a man's life. I'm going on ahead to tell them the news.'

WELCOME BACK

The dawn was breaking over the hills and I stood watching the skyline anxiously. I hadn't been able to sleep. It had been a cold night and there was still no sign of Ben. In the far distance a black dot appeared to be swooping towards me. A bird of some sort, a crow possibly, but it seemed smaller than that. When it got closer it looked uncommonly like a skylark. Thanks to Ben I had got to know quite a bit about birds. And this one looked particularly familiar. It can't be … can't possibly be … Tipsy? But she can't fly. Whatever is she doing in the air?

She landed with a flourish beside me. 'What happened, Tipsy?' I gasped. 'And where's Ben. Is he all right?'

She took a moment to get her breath back and tell me all about it. Tears filled my eyes. The skylark had found her wings again and my beautiful Ben with his thick brown wool had turned himself into a duvet. I couldn't have been more proud.

When Ben got back down the hill to the valley we were all waiting to greet him. A huge jeep was parked near the fence and a man and a girl were making their way up the hill towards Jack. The girl was crying.

I rushed forward and held him as tight as I could. Jacob gave him a huge pat on the back. Owen and Jacuzzi pinned something small and silver to his wool. 'It's a medal,' whispered Jacuzzi excitedly.

'Made out of a recycled spoon,' said Owen solemnly.

'But what's happened?' asked Ben, alarmed. 'What's this all for?'

'You,' I said. 'You and Tipsy. You saved Jack's life.'

'She's called Tiptoe now,' said Ben. He

I nodded at Jacuzzi, who skipped forward carrying the most beautiful necklaces woven from marsh marigolds and wild orchids.

looked behind him and saw that the people had caught up with Jack and were guiding him gently back down the path.

'We are so proud of you,' I said solemnly. 'Both of you. You are a living example of how the different species can work together for the greater good. Ben provided the blanket and Tiptoe the entertainment. Warmth and company. Two vital ingredients for survival.'

I nodded at Jacuzzi, who skipped forward carrying the most beautiful necklaces woven from marsh marigolds and wild orchids. She placed them round their necks. A gaggle of lambs had pushed their way forward to watch what was going on. The bold one who always used to pull Ben's wool was staring open-mouthed at his medal, which was glinting brightly in the morning sun. Behind them a group of sheep, feigning indifference, were pretending not to listen. But I noticed a couple watching curiously, a reluctant admiration in their eyes.

That evening we threw a big party with elderberry wine and buttercup cakes and salad

I presented Ben with my first knitted recycled hat.
It was so small it only covered one ear.

sandwiches garnished with tiny sprigs of parsley. I presented Ben with my first knitted recycled hat. It was so small it only covered one ear.

'I'll finish the other half by next year,' I told him.

Owen nodded in approval.

It sat on his head like a tea cosy.

'Your ears will have to take it in turn,' said Jacuzzi laughing. 'One ear in, one ear out.'

'I love it, Mum,' Ben said.

'And I love you, my beautiful son. I'm so proud of you.'

After supper the same lamb who couldn't keep his eyes off the medal sidled shyly up to Ben.

'We're going to play hide and seek. I don't suppose you want to join us?'

Ben's wool tingled. He swallowed. It was the first time he had ever been asked.

'It's all right,' the lamb was saying. 'I mean we understand if you're not that interested in our silly games.'

'You bet I am!' said Ben.

That night just as he was falling asleep he felt something land on his back. A feather gently brushed against his face. He opened his eyes.

''Night, Ben. Sleep tight.' She settled down in his wool.

He smiled to himself. ''Night, Tiptoe,' he whispered.

HITTING THE HEADLINES

A few days later Owen was sorting through a stack of old magazines when something caught his eye. It was the headline of the front page of the local newspaper.

MAN SAVED BY MYTHICAL CREATURE ON BEN EDRA

19-year-old Jack Lambert, the climber who was reported missing on Ben Edra, has been found alive and well. He was suffering from hypothermia. He admits he was poorly equipped for such a trek and by the evening had run out of supplies and lost all sense of orientation. He claims his life was saved by some sort of creature that kept him warm

A few days later Owen was sorting through a stack of old magazines when something caught his eye.

throughout the night and gave him the strength to make his way back. He can't be sure what it was. It could have been a sheep or a unicorn or even a kind of bird. Was there some benevolent spirit watching over him? Earlier on in the trek he had mislaid his mobile phone and it was later returned to him. He is certainly not the first to have experienced such phenomena. Throughout history there have been various recordings of strange happenings on this mountain for which there has been no scientific explanation. It is perhaps not for nothing that Ben Edra comes from the Gaelic, 'the hill in between'.

But according to Dr Jim Reynolds, a psychiatrist based at Raigmore hospital in Inverness, such experiences should not be taken too literally. 'It is not uncommon for people in an advanced stage of undercooling to drift in and out of consciousness, and in so doing to suffer from such delusions. Added to this, the strange rock formations and desolate nature of this part of the world lend themselves to such imaginings.'

However Lambert insists he didn't imagine it. He claims if it hadn't been for this creature he wouldn't be here today. 'At one point I could have sworn there was this sheep with a bird on its back. Just seeing that did something to me. It gave me a new lease of life.'